BOY, CAN HE DANCE!

written by **Eileen Spinelli**   illustrated by **Paul Yalowitz**

Four Winds Press ❈ *New York*

Maxwell Macmillan Canada   *Toronto*   Maxwell Macmillan International   *New York   Oxford   Singapore   Sydney*

Library of Congress Cataloging-in-Publication Data   Spinelli, Eileen. Boy, can he dance! / story by Eileen Spinelli; pictures by Paul Yalowitz.—1st American ed.   p.   cm.   Summary: Although his father wants him to follow the family tradition and become a chef, a young boy would much rather dance.   ISBN 0-02-786350-6   [1. Dancing—Fiction.   2. Occupations—Fiction.   3. Fathers and sons—Fiction.]   I. Yalowitz, Paul, ill.   II. Title. PZ7.S7566Bo   1993   [E]—dc20   92-12929

A NOTE ON THE ART   The illustrations in this book were first drawn with ebony pencil on bristol plate paper and then colored over with Derwent color pencils. Because the artist is right-handed, he starts drawing on the left side of the paper and moves to the right so that the picture won't smudge. The paper is very smooth, and only the artist knows where that mysterious texture comes from. The illustrations were color-separated and reproduced using four-color process.

*To my children
and their favorite dancing partners*
—E.S.

*To my nephew T.J.—
may he dance forever*
—P. Y.

Many years ago Tony's grandfather had been chef at the City Hotel. He had created graceful ice sculptures. He had designed perfect, pink raspberry molds and white, frosted wedding cakes. He had even learned to cook the mayor's favorite bean soup.

Now Tony's father was chef in the same kitchen of the same hotel.

And when it came time for Tony to begin to think about what he wanted to do with his life, his father said: "Think about food."

"Eating?" asked Tony.

"No, cooking," said Tony's father.

This would have made great sense except for one thing. Tony did not want to think about cooking. He wanted to think about dancing.

Even before Tony learned to walk, he was dancing... an infant dance... kicking his legs and waving his arms so hard that his crib rolled to the other side of the room.

The first day Tony stood up, he started dancing. He danced everywhere. He danced all the time. He danced in the basement and in the attic. He danced at breakfast and in the bathtub. He danced in the backyard and up to the candy store. He even danced on the school bus. That is, until Mr. Wilson, the driver, told him, none too politely, to *sit down!*

"Dancing is fine," Tony's father would say. "I dance myself. With your mother. Once a year. On New Year's Eve." Then, waving his favorite wooden spoon, he would continue, "But I didn't earn my way in the world by dancing. And neither did your grandfather."

And so, early one Saturday morning, Tony's father took Tony to the City Hotel. "If you're going to be a chef when you grow up," he said, "you might as well start learning the business."

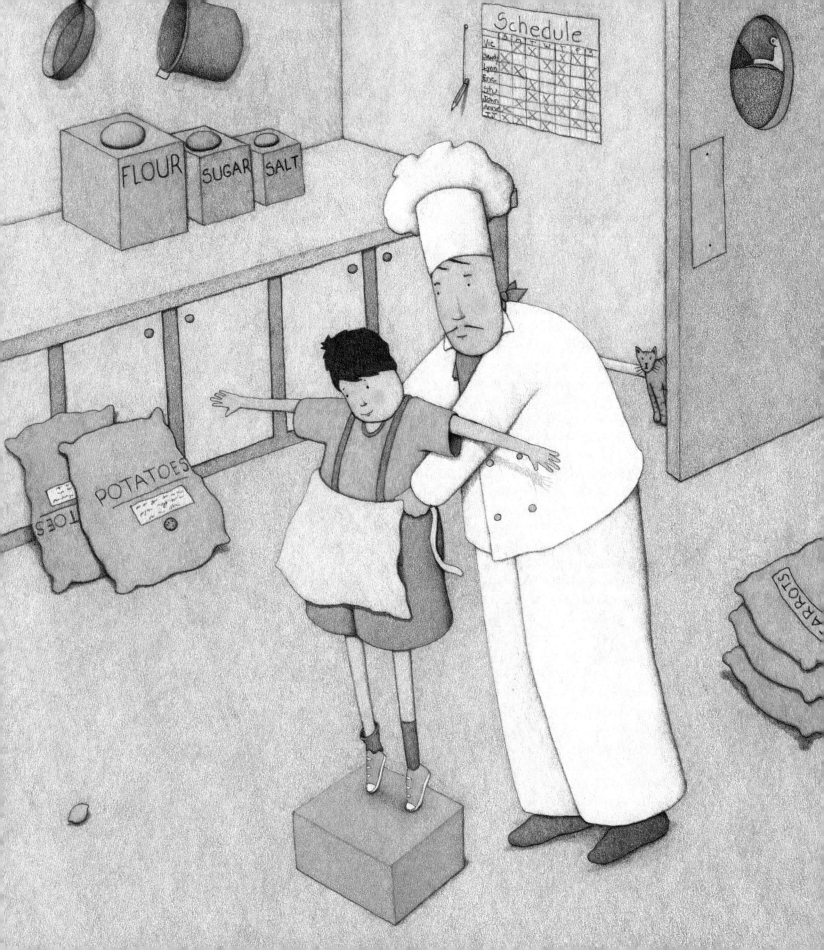

Tony's father dumped a pile of lemons on the table.
"Maybe you should begin by squeezing lemons for the pies."
Tony did not feel like squeezing lemons. But he didn't
want to disappoint his father, either.
And so he began.

Squeeze, squeeze, squeeze.

And the squeezing got him to tapping, and
the tapping got him to dancing.
As he danced he juggled lemons. Tony sailed through the air, juggling

into a waiter carrying a tray of empty dishes.

Crash!

The dishes shattered across the floor.

Plop. Plop. Plop.

Three lemons fell right onto the waiter's head.
"Who is that?" growled the waiter.
"That's my son," sighed Tony's father,
taking Tony by the hand. "Maybe you'd
better chop the carrots for the soup."

lemons... right smack

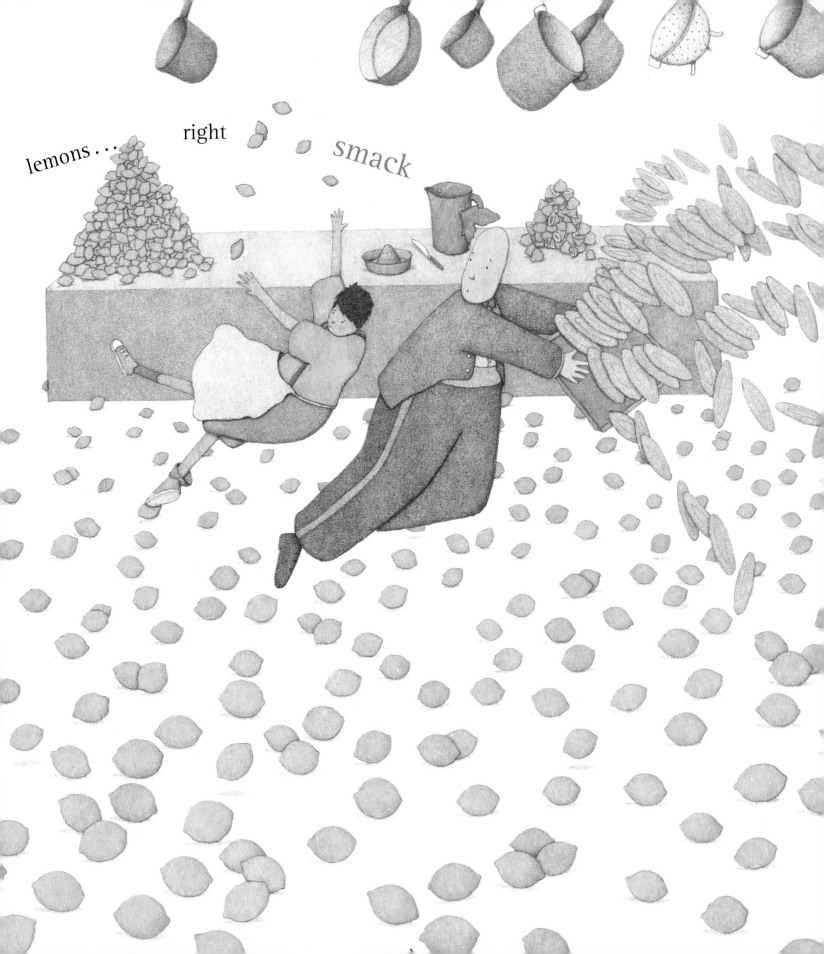

Tony stood in front of the big
chopping-block table and began.
Chop, chop, chop.
And the chopping got him to tapping,
and the tapping got him to dancing.

Round and round the table he danced.

into the woman who brewed the coffee.
"Who is that?" she asked, quite annoyed.
"That's my son," sighed Tony's father.

"Tony," he said, "please peel these potatoes, and please stand still!"

Tony's father dumped a mountain of potatoes at Tony's feet.

Tony did not feel like peeling potatoes, but he didn't want to disappoint his father, either. So he began.

Scrape, scrape, scrape.

And the scraping got him to tapping, and the tapping got him to dancing. Up one side of the potato mountain and down

Right smack into the man who scrubbed pots.

"Who is that?" the man demanded, none too happily.

"That's my son," sighed Tony's father.

He took Tony aside. "This dancing has to stop!"

the other.

"The dancing must go on!" cried the hotel manager, Mr. Casey, bursting into the kitchen. He was clearly upset. And whenever Mr. Casey was upset, he'd burst into the kitchen to grumble, complain, and eat cream puffs.

Biting into a cream puff, he told of his problem. One of the dancers for that night's show had called in sick. "I've tried everywhere to get a replacement. Oh, my head! Oh, my nerves! Oh, pass me another cream puff!"

Tony tugged on Mr. Casey's arm. "I can dance."

Mr. Casey stopped stuffing his mouth. "Who is that?"

"That's my son," sighed Tony's father. "I brought him in to learn to cook."

"Does he really dance?"

"Yup," said the waiter.

"He dances!" exclaimed the woman who brewed the coffee.

"*Boy, does he dance!*" said the man who washed the pots.

With that, Tony jumped up on the table and began dancing. He danced and twirled and kicked and spun until everyone was dizzy.

Mr. Casey looked at Tony's father. "Mind if I borrow your son?"

"Please do!" called the waiter.

That night two hundred people came to the banquet
at the City Hotel. They ate everything that was served,

and many of them said to the waiter, "My compliments
to the chef!" which was music to Tony's father's ears.

But Tony was hearing a different music.
All day he had been practicing with the other dancers.
    Now, with the dinner over, he stood behind the curtain of
the City Hotel's grand stage.
    The orchestra began to play.

As the curtain went up, Tony began to dance.
He *danced* and *twirled*
and *kicked* and *spun* around.

Tony's father watched from the open kitchen door.

The man who ran the dishwasher watched, too. "Who is that?" he asked.

"That's my son," beamed Tony's father...